WIT AND WISDOM

A YEAR'S SUPPLY OF
APHORISMS, INSIGHTS, AND FABLES

By

Harold Raley

TotalRecall Publications, Inc.
1103 Middlecreek
Friendswood, TX 77546
281-992-3131 TEL
www.totalrecallpress.com

Copyright © 2021 by: Harold Raley

ISBN: 978-1-64883-1263
UPC: 6-43977-41263-8

FIRST EDITION
1   2   3   4   5   6   7   8   9   10

For Vicky

Introduction

Many entries in this book are my creations; others are gleanings and adaptations from several languages and cultures. All resonate to my experience.

Aphorisms, witticisms, moral tales, and similar insights are akin to philosophy but with two main differences: first, whereas philosophy reaches a point after lengthy preliminaries, aphorisms and their relatives begin with the point and its immediate human application. Second, whereas philosophy narrate in a major key, these entries play on several registers: humor, irony, paradox, and moral insights that modulate the melody of human life.

According to one of the aphorisms in this book, some of our ideas fare better in other minds. These have served me well as instruction and consolation. Now I release them in the hope that other minds will make even better use of them.

Harold Raley
Houston, Texas 2021

Table of Contents

JANUARY

Day 1. Forgive generously . . .

Forgive generously. The depth of our forgiveness is the depth of our love.

Day 2. What doomsayers predicted . . .

What doomsayers predicted finally happened: the world went to the dogs. But now I hear the dogs are sending it back.

Day 3. Women must be coaxed . . .

Women must be coaxed to come aboard; men must be curbed from going overboard.

Day 4. Some aphorisms . . .

Some aphorisms are so beautifully crafted that we forgive them the inconvenience of not being true.

Day 5. Problems with Relative Truth . . .

> I'm having problems with relative truth. I added two and two and decided to make it come out to five, which was relatively better for me on my tax return. I argued to no avail with the IRS: they still think it's four. Don't they know the answer is what I decide it is?

Day 6. My friend is a liberal . . .

> My friend is a liberal; he believes in equal riots for all unless they come too close to his gated mansion, and he never drives by a flag burning without pulling over to hand out matches.

Day 7. My friend is a conservative . . .

> My friend is a conservative; he believes equality should be restricted to the lower classes and puts democrats in the same category with people who worship snakes.

Day 8. It takes two . . .

> It takes two to make a marriage—maybe three in France—it would be too great a burden for one person to do it alone.

Day 9. A fable . . .

One day a Babylonian commander and his men mocked a Hebrew prophet as he walked along the Tigris River. But he responded to their insults by saying prayers in their name. Then one of his disciples said to the prophet: "Master, you prayed for these Babylonians who mocked you. Why aren't you incensed against them for their hateful words?" The prophet answered: "I can spend only the coins I have in my purse."

The moral: The content of our heart determines how we treat others.

Day 11. For ages . . .

For ages men lived beyond themselves, competing for wealth, territory, and power. Meanwhile, restricted and dominated by men, women had to dwell within a personal space defined by privacy, modesty, and excessive clothing. Then with the suddenness of things that have outlived their time, women emerged from their confinement, shed much of their clothing, and the old ways ended. What the world is coming to now is anybody's guess, everybody's business, and nobody's certainty.

Day 10. The twinkling . . .

> The twinkling stars are cast too high,
> To banish dark and brighten sky,
> But moon by night and sun by day,
> Shed light enough to find our way.

Day 12. Nothing promises . . .

Nothing promises more happiness than love, and nothing breaks its promises more often. Perfect love is perfect happiness, but because we are imperfect, and our mortal life brief, complete happiness remains an unreachable ideal in this world. That's why we need a Heaven.

Day 13. Love is . . .

Love is recognizing someone we meet for the first time, or after a long time, as the person destined from the beginning to fill the emptiness in our life.

Day 14. The Canine Cult . . .

The Canine Cult is without doubt the fastest growing movement in the world today, and it involves a new and alarming form of human slavery. You see it everywhere: sweatered and festively ribboned dogs leading shabby humans around on leashes. And in the upscale neighborhoods some already have luxury automobiles and chauffeurs to drive them to posh places. If attendance continues to decline in churches and temples, this cult could soon surpass some of our established religions. I'm here to warn you that something must be done before it's too late for humanity. Otherwise, we shall have to learn to walk on all fours and bark. And how good are you at retrieving sticks and terrorizing mailmen?

Day 15. It is sad . . .

It is sad to live long enough to see old errors being recycled as new ideas. We learn almost nothing from mistakes others make and very little from our own. But maybe there is a positive side to our forgetfulness. If we dwelt only on all our wrong steps, we might soon become too cautious to take any right ones.

Day 16. Eve became frustrated . . .

Eve became frustrated with her love life and asked Adam if he could turn over a new leaf.

Day 17. Who are God's chosen . . .

Who are God's chosen people? I would say it's anybody who's made it this far alive.

Day 18. Live in such a way . . .

Live in such a way that those who praise your virtues speak truth and those who accuse you of vice spread slander.

Day 19. He swam the sea . . .

He swam the sea but drowned ashore. Some people are better at fighting the war than living the peace.

Day 20. We tolerate . . .

We tolerate the world's great evils but complain about minor irritants. Some evils are so old and vast that we mistake them for the world itself; it is the local pests that anger us.

Day 21. English . . .

English: A pile of words, mostly foreign, that become English as soon as we mispronounce them properly. Then the mixture requires a dash of grammar and spelling that is beyond the ability of ordinary mortals to master, especially native English speakers. But it all becomes real English only when we spice it with appropriate vulgarities. Everyone knows you can't really curse in a foreign language. For gut-level blasphemy only our nasty little four-letter Anglo-Saxon words will do.

Day 22. I heard . . .

I heard that in earth's Golden Age some people grumbled about the price of gold, others disliked its yellow color, and still others complained about its weight. I'm relieved; if people could find nothing to complain about, the world would probably go belly up.

Day 23. A Fable . . .

The villagers of an ancient kingdom caught a thief in the act and decided that at nightfall they would drown him in a nearby lake. Then tying him to a post and covering his head with a cloth, they went off to work their fields.

A curious shepherd happened along with his sheep and loosening the cloth, asked the thief why he was bound.

"Because I would not take money from these evil people."

"But why should they offer you money, and why would you not take it?"

"I am devoted wholly to pious contemplation of the Almighty and consider material things unworthy," he explained. "Knowing this, these godless men were trying to contaminate my soul with money."

"Then let me take your place," the greedy shepherd urged, "I will take their money and you shall be free to go your way."

Whereupon, they exchanged places, covering the shepherd's head with the cloth. That night, thinking him the thief, the villagers ignored his muffled cries and threw the shepherd into the lake. But the next morning they were astonished to see the thief alive and with a flock of sheep.

"How is it that you are alive and where did you get those sheep?" they asked.

"From the lake. Therein dwells a mighty genie who rewards in like manner all who dive into his waters to honor him. These sheep are proof of his generosity, as you can plainly see."

Spurred by greed, the astonished villagers promptly jumped into the lake themselves, and the thief became the owner of their village.

Moral: Stupidity and greed make short work of many human schemes.

Day 24. The French and English . . .

French and English armies used to slaughter themselves in endless wars. The mayhem continues but now the casualties are their respective languages. No one abuses the English language like the French, and the way English speakers mistreat French borders on cruel and unusual linguistic punishment. To speak French, you must form your lips into a permanent pucker as though ready to spit and hope you can find an occasional consonant to which to anchor the slippery French nasals. But these facial contortions seem indecent to native English speakers, who prefer to talk by moving their lips as little as possible. As for English, the worst thing you can do is to pronounce its imported French words as the French do. Most Americans think that to speak proper French—or any other foreign language, including British English—is somehow unamerican. The British confine French to drawing up formal treaties after rescuing France from another defeat by the Germans. Americans believe that the proper purpose of French is to order wine, escargot, or croissants and discuss decadent literature in quaint little sidewalk cafés.

Day 25. We do not hold grudges . . .

We do not hold grudges; they hold us. To bear a grudge is human, to release it, sensible, maybe divine.

Day 26. If you tell . . .

> If you tell your secrets to others sworn to secrecy, they will tell them as readily as you have. Which means there are only two foolproof ways to keep secrets: first and preferably, have none; second and without exception, do not tell the ones you have.

Day 27. Common criminals . . .

> Common criminals serve terms in prison; great ones serve terms in Washington. Many of the latter are repeat offenders.

Day 28. To forgive . . .

> To forgive is to release both the offended and the offender from bondage. But forgiveness requires of both parties a generosity of spirit that not all possess, and even fewer in matching degrees.

Day 29. The Law of creation . . .

> The Law of creation: nothing is finished for good until it is entirely good.

Day 30. Ask not of God . . .

Ask not of God what you can do for yourself, nor entreat heaven for what you can do without. God does not cater to our whims but always responds in a way that is proper for us.

Day 31. Thank God . . .

Thank God for unanswered prayers. Heaven help us if he granted all we ask for. The world would bloat with undying people; doctors, hospitals, and pharmaceutical companies would go bankrupt; the hereafter would be canceled; and probably heaven itself would be foreclosed and its celestial properties put up for sale.

FEBRUARY

Day 32. The first time . . .

The first time you hear Spanish, it has the staccato rhythm of a woodpecker sculpting a marble nude. You are amazed that humans can speak so fast. When you get into it you learn it has the verbal complexity of Latin but without the cases and declensions that were created to torture generations of future students. Then there's Texas Spanish. If conventional Spanish has too many verbs, the Texas variety has none. You can claim reasonable fluency in it if you can count to ten and order beer, tacos, and tamales. Without verbs, as noted above; no self-respecting Texan would stoop so low as to learn them. After all, they point out, they fought a war to pronounce Spanish their way.

Day 33. Shouldn't we . . .

Shouldn't we live each working day like a miniature lifetime, rising with the morning sun to love, reflect, pray, work, play, serve, sing, and give thanks until day is done, then go to our rest with gratitude for today and faith in tomorrow?

Day 34. The saints . . .

> The saints are not noisy or hasty, but at peace with themselves and others, and on time in their tasks. Therein lies a mystery; in ways that defy understanding, time expands to accommodate the saintly but shrinks to frustrate the sinful.

Day 35. Streams . . .

> Streams, like people, are usually swiftest and noisiest at their shallowest.

Day 36. Noise . . .

> Noise and haste are sin's close kin. For a complete list of their relatives consult the Bible or draw up your own likely list.

Day 37. Many of us . . .

> Many of us pursue wealth and then must protect it. Few seek knowledge, but it protects us. Money has its virtues and must not to be disparaged, but knowledge better serves us.

Day 38. A Fable . . .

A farmer was passing by an abandoned well when he heard a cry for help. Looking in, he saw a man standing waist-deep in the stagnant water amidst spiders and crawly creatures.

"Can I hep you, mister?" he called out.

"You certainly may, my good man! I am a professor, and on my way to lecture at the university chanced to misstep and fall down this well shaft."

"Well, sir, don't you fret none. Jist you wait a little bit while I go git some ropes and a feller to hep me pull you out."

"Well and good, but I must tell you that your language is atrocious. You must learn to speak correctly."

The farmer paused then said: "Well, Mr. perfessor, I reckon you'll jist have to stay down there for a spell while I go learn how to talk good."

And he went on his way.

Moral: It is unwise to put secondary matters ahead of primary problems.

Day 39. We declare . . .

We declare ourselves undeserving of praise so that others will praise us twice. Hypocrisy and modesty are old acquaintances.

Day 40. Many of the problems . . .

Many of the problems of freedom can be solved by more freedom. Freedom is risky, but it is better than any alternatives I can think of.

Day 41. When people . . .

When people praise us, don't we secretly think they are telling us what we've already told ourselves? How fortunate that others cannot see our thoughts. Or is it?

Day 42. Flattery . . .

Flattery is normal in romance, but elsewhere it is usually either a ploy to gain favor or a dainty form of contempt—or both. But flattery continues alive and well because nearly all of us like to be . . . well, flattered.

Day 43. Maturity . . .

Maturity comes not at a certain age but at the point in life when we stop acting cute and start doing right.

Day 44. Meditation on a flood . . .

Meditation on a flood: There is a tide in the affairs of men, which, taken at the flood, leads on . . . to a soggy mess and big hikes in insurance costs.

Day 45. Debates . . .

Debates are usually a waste of everybody's time. Nothing was ever learned by taking sides. The victim of these squabbles is usually truth itself drawn and quartered by both sides.

Day 46. No one . . .

No one was ever improved by envy. If you cannot be great by the standards of this world, do not be lessened by envying those who are.

Day 47. Those without aim . . .

Those without aim would make you the same. Idleness is to our humanity what rust is to machinery.

Day 48. What is time?

What is time? St. Augustine said that if you did not ask him, he knew, but if you asked him, he could not say. Einstein and others have taught us that time is flexible, but its quantum secrets still elude us, and the more we learn the less certain we are about the little we do know.

Day 49. Reality . . .

Reality is the sum of our individual perspectives. The so-called "objective" point of view, meaning things seen from nowhere and by nobody, is a false perspective of reality, useful in the abstract but the mother of many errors at other levels.

Day 50. Our life . . .

Our life began before we did. We did not create the languages we speak, the ideals we hold, the faiths we profess, the customs we observe, the numbers we sum, or the music we hum. Long before we were born, much of our life was already up and running.

Day 51. Religion . . .

Religion: the broadest of truths organized by the narrowest of minds.

Day 52. We are the future . . .

We the future of people who lived before us, the fulfillment or failure of what they strove for. And for good or ill, we shall be the past of those yet unborn. We are linked to the whole skein of human time. We belong to one another, to the living and the departed, to the abolished and lost, to those who are and those who will be. All are part of the human chain of life, and to diminish it is to diminish oneself, and to enrich it is to enrich humanity.

Day 53. Beware . . .

Beware of tolerant people who will tolerate everything but your intolerance of the intolerable. Tolerance is the watchword of our time, but the truth is that we are as intolerant as our ancestors were, only of different things and different people. In turn, the younger generations have replaced our intolerances with their own, and to our dismay, often we find our own tolerant selves included on their list of intolerable things.

Day 54. In love . . .

In love and business avoid people with more problems than you have. Can we reasonably expect those unable to manage their own affairs in these areas to be any better at managing ours?

Day 55. A Fable . . .

A penniless man trudged along a lonely road despairing of life as he peeled and ate his last apple.

"Where, dear God, shall I find my next meal?" he moaned. "I am the most wretched of men without help or hope in this desolate land."

At that moment he heard a noise, and turning, saw a woman, shabbier than himself, feeding her starving infant the peelings he had dropped.

Moral: If we can walk, see, and speak, there are others in worse condition and needful of our help.

Day 56. Words . . .

Words amplify or hinder creation. With a word we can lift spirits heavenward, and with another, consign them to hell. Our words are not divine, but they have power and can interfere with divine power if we infuse them with doubt or evil intent. This is why Jesus could do few miracles in skeptical Nazareth.

Day 57. Hunger . . .

Hunger makes any bread delicious. Man does not live by bread alone, but that does not mean he can live without it.

Day 58. Time . . .

Time does not pass; we do. We mark time with clocks, calendars, and celestial movements, but these are mere human calculations and do not mean that time itself passes. For if does, then where does it go? And where does replacement time come from? The evidence argues that time is timeless and timelessly remains, but we pass away.

Day 59. A good man . . .

A good man and a good wife overcome great strife. A single person may fail, a partnership collapse, but a durable marriage bond has a strength multiplied to a much higher degree than either person alone.

Day 60. As one . . .   (Leap Year extra)

As one they dwell
If all is well.
What one declares
The other shares.

(A rimed way of saying that happy couples generally agree)

MARCH

Day 61. Happy wife . . .

Happy wife, happy life. As the popular saying goes, "if Momma's not happy, nobody's happy." Conversely, if she is happy, then usually everybody around her is too.

Day 62. Everything human . . .

Everything human is fragile and easily forgotten. Nature endows animals with instincts necessary for making their way. But we humans lack instincts and are dependent on our elders for the exceptionally long periods of time it takes us to learn complex languages, skills, and technics. No wonder forgetfulness and laziness have destroyed as many cultures as hostile armies.

Day 63. Well-meaning people . . .

Well-meaning people speak much of the end of time, but what could fill the timeless void except more time? Often what we most assert we least understand.

Day 64. Evil . . .

Evil is not the opposite of good but the absence of good. To think that good and evil are locked in a cosmic war elevates evil to a level it does not deserve.

Day 65. There are people . . .

There are people who make it their business to see that God remains manacled to the Bible.

Day 66. Truth . . .

Truth is like a lost coin: you turn everything upside down and inside out searching for it, then one day there it is: in plain sight right where you left it.

Day 67. "With God . . ."

"With God all things are possible," say the Scriptures, billboards, and well-meaning people. But does it mean that God could also do evil things if he chose? Of course not, but it shows why we must be prepared to defend our faith with sound reasoning, not wishful thinking.

Day 68. A Fable . . .

An egg fell from an eagle's aery and landing on soft grass, rolled intact into a ground bird's nest. The mother bird nudged it next to her own small eggs and sat faithfully on them until all hatched. Rude neighbors pecked and ridiculed the eaglet, but the mother bird loved her odd chick, and as mothers will, protected it and taught it to scratch for grubs and worms.

One day he told his mother that he had a desire to fly.

"Banish that unnatural thought," she scolded him. "We are ground birds, not those odd sky birds who risk their lives."

The eaglet obeyed but at times he envied the sky birds.

One day a great eagle perched high in a nearby tree.

"Youngster," he called down, "why are you down there on the ground scratching for worms in the dirt?"

"Because, sir, I live here. I am a ground bird."

"No, you are not. I know eagles, and you are an eagle."

"But eagles fly, and I cannot. I am a ground bird."

"Would you let me teach you to fly and find real meat?"

"I am afraid, sir. My mother says I should not think about such things. We are ground birds."

"I shall come back tomorrow to help if you are ready," said the great eagle as he soared off. The next day he returned, and the next, but each time the eaglet was too frightened to try its wings. Finally, the great eagle flew away never to return.

"I am a ground bird," the eaglet said sadly as he scratched in the dirt for grubs. "I can be only what I was born to be."

Moral: It is risky to become who you really are, but tragic not to make the effort.

Day 69. To the wise . . .

To the wise, the world is always more than they know; to the simpleminded, the world is not worth knowing.

Day 70. Success . . .

Success has an army of admirers, but failure is a shunned exile.

Day 71. News item . . .

News item: Man goes shopping, finds 15,000 bees in his car when he returns. Remarkably brave of him to take the time to count them, don't you think?

Day 72. We are pleased . . .

We are pleased with people who envy us but seldom with those we envy.

Day 73. Women confidently claim . . .

Women confidently claim they understand men, while men cheerfully declare that women baffle them. But to judge by the emotional wreckage each gender causes the other, it seems that both are equally skilled at dealing misery, particularly in matters of the heart.

Day 74. The hardest people . . .

The hardest people to kill are the dead tyrants who still tyrannize the world with their ideologies.

Day 75. Take care . . .

Take care of your body before forty and it will take care of you after forty. There are exceptions, but as always, exceptions confirm the rule.

Day 76. It is hard . . .

It is hard to forgive those who have no need of our advice.

Day 77. A Fable . . .

A rich merchant named Yuxel chanced to overhear a conversation between brothers Fate and Death.

"I am weary" Death confided to his brother. "The plague in this country has allowed me no rest these many months."

"And expect none for the remainder of this year," Fate responded. "My list is long with names of those fated to die."

"So is mine," Death sighed. "But why are you here?"

"I must verify the whereabouts of a man named Yuxel. He is on my list. He resides in this city, but some uncertainty remains about his exact location."

Terrified, Yuxel rushed home and ordered his servants to prepare his carriage. Then with his gold and treasures aboard he raced away as fast as his horses could run to a distant city where he hoped to hide from Death. But no sooner had he arrived than he came upon Death and Fate conversing in a park.

"So, brother, we meet again," Death said to Fate. "What business brings you hither?"

"I have found the man named Yuxel. He is here where he was destined to be. And why are you here?"

"For the same man. He is also on my list."

At that very hour Yuxel died as he was fated to do.

Moral: According to the ancient fatalism of the Eastern world, "Mankind's fate cannot be altered. What must be, will be."

Day 78. If I were . . .

If I were describing the sexes in meteorological terms, men would be the weather, women, the climate. The weather shines, storms, and blows in daily variation. The climate changes slowly, but in time it alters the world.

Day 79. According to Holy Writ . . .

According to Holy Writ our body is the temple of the soul and thus deserves to be cared for morally and physically. But instead
of respecting the body as the temple of our life, why do many contemporary believers treat theirs so shabbily? Shouldn't we treat the Creator's greatest creation with the greatest respect?

Day 80. Of course . . .

Of course, the lower classes are equals, but have you noticed they're starting to move into our neighborhood? Can't they be equal over there where they're supposed to live?

Day 81. Men conquer . . .

Men conquer, women captivate. Debate continues about which gender has won the larger empire.

Day 82. Philosopher . . .

Philosopher Miguel de Unamuno once remarked that a person is worth more than the entire universe. His words alternately sound to me like base nonsense or uncommon insight. Rationally, I dismiss them, but spiritually I sense in his words a wisdom that surpasses the keenest human intellects. His thinking annoys me like no other, yet I would rather fight with him than agree with many other thinkers.

Day 83. Courage . . .

Courage, courtesy, and integrity are gifts we give ourselves. And unlike tangible valuables, these gifts cannot be stolen or taken from us.

Day 84. A Fable . . .

A thief stole a sheep, tied a rope about its neck, and led it away. But another thief cut the rope and ran off with the twice-stolen sheep. Later, still fretting over his loss, the first thief came upon a man trying to retrieve an object from a murky river.

"Sir," the man said to the thief, "I dropped a box containing a hundred gold coins in the river. I cannot go in for it myself lest thieves who infest this region open the pen and rob me of my unguarded flock. But if you can retrieve the box for me whilst I keep watch over the animals, I will give you ten coins as a reward."

The thief was delighted. Ten gold coins are worth much more than my stolen sheep, he said to himself. Besides, he thought slyly, perhaps I can snatch all the coins, since the shepherd cannot leave the sheepfold to chase me. Then he removed his shoes and clothes and jumped in the river for the box. Whereupon the shepherd—in reality, the thief who had stolen his sheep—ran away with his sheep, clothes, shoes, and money, leaving his victim naked, destitute, and without the imaginary box of coins.

Moral: Sheep are not the only naïve creatures fleeced.

Day 85. As a professor . . .

As a professor of foreign languages, I can tell you that women
are better than men at learning them. I wondered why until it
occurred to me that since men don't listen when women
speak to them in English, they might get their attention if they
tried another language. It's not God's fault that the
experiment hasn't worked out.

Day 86. A man's concept . . .

A man's concept of housecleaning: make sure everything is
put back in its proper disorder.

Day 87. There is . . .

There is always a fine line between what we own and what
owns us.

Day 88. An elevated life . . .

An elevated life is built on elevated thoughts. And the same
is true of a life based on degraded thoughts. The biblical
affirmation sums it well: "As a man thinketh in his heart, so
is he."

Day 89. Opportunity . . .

Opportunity usually picks those who have prepared themselves for it. It may not always come to the prepared, but seldom will it bother with the unprepared.

Day 90. Forgive readily . . .

Forgive readily but be as prudent with repaired friendships as sailors are with repaired vessels. Put limits on your resumed trust: a recovered alcoholic should not be put in charge of a wine shop, nor a former embezzler entrusted with company finances.

Day 91. The true measure . . .

The true measure of nobility lies in the respect with which people treat those too humble to expect it or too arrogant to care. This kind of respect depends less on another's character than on one's own. True respect for others is rooted in self-respect, not in self-righteousness or another's prestige.

APRIL

Day 92. When romantic love . . .

> When romantic love dies it cannot be resurrected, though deeper and more enduring forms of love may replace it. Caught up in the euphoria of romantic love, no one doubts that it will last forever,
> but its very intensity may cause it to burn out unless sturdier varieties of love arise to support it.

Day 93. I don't like . . .

> I don't like to speak ill of anyone, but I overheard somebody say he's a lawyer.

Day 94. My liberal friend . . .

> My liberal friend opposes capitalism but sees nothing wrong with having more of it than anybody else.

Day 95. My conservative senator . . .

> My conservative senator is on a mission to put first things first in Washington, but not exactly in that order.

Day 96. A Fable . . .

A merchant owned a talking monkey admired for its antics and clever stories. One day the merchant told the monkey that he was leaving on a journey to his pet's native country.

"Master," the monkey said, "I have served you faithfully these many years. Now I ask that you allow me to return with you to my country and kindred."

"I'll do no such thing," answered the merchant. "Not only do you entertain me but also attract customers to my business with your clever tricks and delightful tales."

"Then will you at least visit my relatives in the forest and tell them what became of me?"

The merchant agreed and left on his journey. When his business was finished, he remembered the request and visited the monkey relatives. But when he told the family about him, their elder leader suddenly fell at his feet apparently dead. Back home he reported the sad incident to his monkey, whereupon he, too, fell at his feet, also seemingly dead. The merchant laid his pet by an open window where it soon revived and spoke:

"Master, what you took for a disaster was in fact a transmitted message from our tribal elder about how I was to escape." Then he said goodbye and he scampered back home.

Moral: Many things are not what they seem but messages above our understanding.

Day 97. A little knowledge . . .

A little knowledge is a dangerous thing, so Alexander Pope tells us, but surpassing knowledge can be lethal; of the few who have attained it in this world, some have paid for its possession with their life.

Day 98. Welcome . . .

Welcome the company of persons of merit and accomplishment greater than yours so that you may learn from their example. But this can happen only when your desire for knowledge and admiration for exemplary achievement are stronger than pride in your own talents and accomplishments and greater than your envy of those more advanced.

Day 99. History justifies . . .

History justifies the winners by blaming the losers.

Day 100. Hungry

A hungry stomach knows no logic.

Day 101. We do not . . .

We do not pursue our ideals; they pursue us, and once on our trail, chase us like the hounds of heaven. Our destiny is relentless, but we may be late in life before we recognize it for what it is.

Day 102. We have heard . . .

We have heard it said that if one has been a part of the problem, one cannot be a part of the solution. But this is not always true: if one is repentant and willing to make amends and correct mistakes, then that very person may be better suited for the task than anyone else. The worst offenders sometimes become the stoutest champions of what they once opposed.

Day 103. In matters . . .

In matters of your heart, give your head the last word. But where others are concerned, speak from the heart. Our heart does not see our own problems clearly, but it is usually a dependable counselor to others.

Day 104. Most arsonists . . .

Most arsonists are men, but women can also start fires if it's time to cook a man's goose.

Day 105. If the world . . .

If the world prevents you from doing the great things you dream, then dream of doing the good things you can.

Day 106. If you are . . .

If you are not who you dream of being, then dream of being who you can be. Second choices sometimes prove to be a better option than our first preference.

Day 107. An enduring human error . . .

An enduring human error: to assume virtue in the poor and malice in the rich.

Day 108. Religious believers . . .

Religious believers generally agree on the broad
fundamentals but divide over the lesser secondaries. It is true
as said that the Devil is at his best—that is, his worst—in the
details.

Day 109. If you would . . .

If you would paint beauty in your art,
You must start with beauty in your heart.
(Art is born of the yearning to portray what yearns to be
revealed.)

Day 110. Humanity's . . .

Humanity's most persistent error is claiming enlightenment
in areas where light does not go. Where our small perimeter
of light ends, the vast darkness of our ignorance begins.

Day 111. Intelligence . . .

Intelligence without morality is like a prostitute: she will
service any client for money, just as amoral intelligence will
serve any cause for pay.

Day 112. When we eat . . .

When we eat too much, something is eating us. The problems we cannot resolve we try to digest instead.

Day 113. The poet

The poet Milton wrote poetry without rhyme; lesser talents wrote rhyme without poetry.

Day 114. When people say . . .

When people say, "you haven't changed a bit," you have; when they say, "you still have it," you don't; when they start calling you "young man," you aren't; when students start telling you, "you remind me of my grandfather," they are probably thinking of a dead man and wondering why you aren't.

Day 115. To be truly original . . .

To be truly original you must be true to your origins. But this means considerably more than just the place and people where you were born.

Day 116. A Fable . . .

A learned man set out to learn more. At first, he attended the sessions of a celebrated teacher in his city. But the learned man soon recognized much foolishness and many errors in his teachings and became disillusioned.

"I must find a more advanced teacher," he said to himself and went on to another city where he was admitted by a master with dozens of disciples. At first, the learned man appreciated the lessons but soon decided that the Master could teach him little more than he already knew. And he journeyed on in his search.

Finally, he came upon a teacher speaking to a single student. "He must be very great scholar to admit only a single student."

But when asked, the teacher refused to admit him.

"But why not, esteemed master? I know much already and desire to study under a greater scholar to add to my knowledge."

"My response is implied in your explanation, which tells me that you have not yet understood the most fundamental lesson."

"And what, sir, is that?" he asked, offended by the rebuff.

"Your motive is vanity when it should be service to your fellow man. Therefore, return to your city and teach those less advanced than you. In that way you may acquire an understanding of service to mankind, which is the foundation of all true knowledge."

Moral: Remember that you are the messenger, not the message.

Day 117. Beware . . .

>Beware the trap that thou hast set,
>Lest thou be snared in thine own net.
>Moral and mental lapses can destroy our best-laid schemes—
>and us in the process.

Day 118. He never . . .

>He never confessed his secrets. His wife was with him right up to the end.

Day 119. Before family . . .

>Before family reunions my mother used to remind me to be nice to people we couldn't stand.

Day 120. Like the wind . . .

>Like the wind, adversity snuffs out small loves but fuels great passions. Hence, whatever you do, do with your main strength if you would have it matter and endure.

Day 121. Upon being . . .

Upon being honored for his landmark studies in metaphysical anthropology, the eminent author responded: "I have done what I could, but my wife has achieved much more. I wrote books on theories of human reality, but she conceived, bore, and guided several real persons to responsible maturity. Hers is the greater accomplishment."

MAY

Day 122. Death clarifies . . .

Death clarifies at once who a person was or failed to be. Only at death when all is stilled and debauchery and dissipation have ended, do we sense the underlying human greatness a derelict person forfeited. At such moments, a corpse sends a message that is more powerful and significant than many preachments about the worth and meaning of human life.

Day 123. It is hard . . .

It is hard to forgive people who bore us, but even harder to forgive those we bore.

Day 124. Some sins . . .

Some sins are more forgivable than those we commit trying to hide them. For much of our life many of us are untroubled by sins safely hidden. Only in full maturity do we come face to face with the full horror of wrongdoing regardless of whether known or unknown.

Day 125. Education . . .

Education isn't everything, but neither are you, and that's why you need it.

Day 126. We are upset . . .

We are upset with those who do not respect us and unnerved by those who respect us more than we deserve.

Day 127. The company . . .

The company we avoid tell as much about us as the company we   keep.

Day 128. To insist . . .

To insist on always being right assures that we shall often be wrong. Unwillingness to admit an error is already an error.

Day 129. Intelligent people . . .

Intelligent people build nations; clever people destroy them; common people save them.

Day 130. If we resist . . .

If we resist our temptations, often it is because they are weak, but sometimes it's because people are watching us.

Day 131. People can . . .

People can always be more or less than they are, able to rise towards the angels or fall towards the apes. It is a human option not available to other creatures. A tiger is forever condemned to being a tiger; humans are condemned to choose who they will be.

Day 132. The truths . . .

The truths an enemy tells us to our face are often more infuriating than the lies he spreads behind our back.

Day 133. Chance . . .

Chance is the wild card of creation. It comes without warning out of nowhere to overrule fate, disrupt destiny, and transform our life. We never know when, how, or if it will come, only that it may at any minute.

Day 134. Consider . . .

Consider Epictetus' ancient advice: if you aim to be good, begin by confessing that you are bad.

Day 135. Men . . .

Men invent gadgets, women invent themselves.

Day 136. God created . . .

God seems to have created everything but sarcasm; that part he left to humans.

Day 137. Mind . . .

Mind what you pray for: some things and people we think we cannot live without we discover later we cannot live with.

Day 138. Exile . . .

Exile was a nightmarish punishment in ancient times, second in severity only to death itself. But today nothing seems better to countless Americans than to abandon the community where they have raised families, built friendships, and had a career for a distant paradise perhaps without family, friends, or career. In my travels I have come across Americans living abroad in the most unlikely places, cut off from their homeland and often unable to speak the local language. Yet those I met claimed to be happy, boasting that they could live there for so little. I missed their point; I prefer places where I can live for so much.

Day 139. Few . . .

Few are bothered by whom we hate, but many are disturbed by whom we love.

Day 140. We are . . .

We are all a threat to people we never met.

Day 141. Know . . .

Know the reasonable order of things: seek advice from the wise, money from the generous, and protection from the powerful.

Day 142. There is always . . .

There is always a rock handy if we mean to stone a man, or a lawyer around if we decide to sue him instead.

Day 143. How many . . .

How many brave people would be cowards if only they had the courage?

Day 144. To win . . .

To win the favor of powerful people, ask them do you a favor.

Day 145. It is better . . .

It is better to ask as a favor what you could demand with an order.

Day 146. Some of your thoughts . . .

Some of your thoughts may work better in another mind.

Day 147. If our passions . . .

If our passions are too weak, we accomplish little; if too strong, they destroy us. Passion is as necessary to our life as fuel is to an engine: both are dangerous if mishandled, but without them both man and motor are powerless.

Day 148. Do not take advice . . .

Do not take advice about death very seriously. Nobody you can talk to has experienced it.

Day 149. Wicked people . . .

Wicked people sometimes do good deeds. I suppose they are curious to see how the other side lives.

Day 150. Always tell . . .

Always tell the truth, particularly if your memory is poor.

Day 151. He was halfway . . .

He was halfway to being a Robin Hood. He had already mastered the part about robbing the rich.

Day 152. The wisest . . .

The wisest among us do not limit things to a single definition. For the same object can be a weapon, a work of art, an icon, a historical artifact, a tool, a chemical composite, or almost anything else that people understand it to be. Creation is packed with possibilities. Our job—and privilege—is to discover some of them.

Day 153. Dead fish . . .

Dead fish and dirty deeds soon float to the surface.

JUNE

Day 154. We admire . . .

We admire virtue but live with vice.

Day 155. To be . . .

To be a creative person, you cannot be entirely rooted in this world.

Day 156. Forget it . . .

Forget it if you had hoped to come back and do things right in the next life. The Chinese have passed a law forbidding reincarnation.

Day 157. Despite . . .

Despite heroic efforts by the rich and glamourous to stay young, age has the last word. Cosmetics and surgery can disguise and delay, but they cannot repeal.

Day 158. Just think . . .

Just think how generous misers are: they scrimp and save, deny themselves everything, and then die and leave their wealth for others to spend.

Day 159. Art reveals . . .

Art reveals realities that common vision does not see.

Day 160. Isn't it time . . .

Isn't it time somebody told the truth about mountains? They displace good farmland, have awful roads, and once you reach the top the only way to go is down.

Day 161. An enemy . . .

An enemy pointed out one of my faults. I was relieved that he overlooked several others I could have told him about.

Day 162. A Fable . . .

A man was beating a dog.

"Why are you beating that dog? a passerby asked him.

"Because he would not sit when I ordered him to."

"Is there a reason why the dog should sit?"

"Of course, there is," the man responded, irritated by the questions. "I am the dog's master, and the animal's duty is to obey me. That is reason enough, if you must know."

The passerby then addressed the dog in canine speech.

"Do you accept the reason the man gives for beating you?"

"Not at all. The real reason is that it bothers him to be led about by one better than he."

Moral: Know all the facts before judging; what seems plausible to one, may be equally or more implausible from another perspective.

Day 163. We all have . . .

We all have thoughts we are ashamed of, but also others that probably are ashamed of us.

Day 164. I don't trust . . .

I don't trust babies; they remind me of humans.

Day 165. People say . . .

People say that the only reliable prophecies are those that became history, but I would say a better criterion is whether they came true. For not everything in history is true, and much that happened is not history.

Day 166. A noted philosopher . . .

A noted philosopher said that entire countries have periodic bouts of insanity. Another described a wave effect in history that predictably lifts societies to intellectual peaks, then plunges them into dark mental valleys. I hope to say more on the matter when there is enough light to see what I am doing.

Day 167. A Fable . . .

The chief of an equatorial tribe was taken to a great city and asked his impressions of its broad streets and busy two-way traffic. For a long time, the chief stood looking in silence before turning back to his hosts. But instead of the expected expressions of awe, he exhibited sorrow and described his sympathy for the busy throngs. He pointed out that the pedestrians were surely lost. A road on which people were rushing in opposite directions had to be a sign of their distress and an indication that they did not know where they were going or which direction to take to get there.

Moral: Probably the chief did not understand many things about the great city, but was his perception really wrong?

Day 168. Paleontologists . . .

Paleontologists have discovered that the earliest humans were already into drugs and intoxicants. It seems that as soon as our ancestors had a mind, they began looking for ways to lose it.

Day 169. Many things . . .

Many things in America remind us of Europe, but only superficial things in Europe remind us of America. The fabric of American civilization is woven from a single democratic thread of the common people of Europe, unlike the European tapestry which consists of several strands: Roman, medieval, aristocratic, monarchical, Renaissance, Reformation, Enlightenment, and democratic. And what both have been, so they continue to be: America is what you see on the surface of history; Europe, what you discover in its depths. Common people came to America; the aristocrats remained in Europe. We are not yet sure which, if either, got the better of the bargain.

Day 170. Our destination . . .

Our destination defines our journey, but only in retrospect; we cannot be certain of where we have gone until we get there and look back.

Day 171. Absence . . .

Absence sharpens real love; practice dulls it.

Day 172. In America . . .

In America it is bad form to boast of one's talents but nearly always proper to exaggerate one's shortcomings. The first custom is commonly observed almost everywhere in the world. The second is more common in America, and along with the tendency to grin for photographs and make mother-in-law jokes, is hard for many nationalities to understand.

Day 173. The less . . .

The less people know, the more they repeat it.

Day 174. Our intuition . . .

Our intuition first tells our heart what logic must then prove to our mind.

Day 175. The way . . .

The way to be a bore is to overtell the story. The way to keep the attention of others is to ask them about themselves, be patient to listen, and most of all, remember what they said.

Day 176. Wisdom . . .

> True wisdom is the willingness to learn from all people. Everyone knows things that we do not. Learn from their experience.

Day 177. The fickle twins . . .

> The fickle twins called luck and chance usually vanish the minute we count on them.

Day 178. Adam . . .

> Adam was the first poet: He gushed poetically when he saw Eve for the first time, then named the things and creatures in the Garden. And God honored his words by accepting them.

Day 179. "Human nature" . . .

> "Human nature" is a contradiction in terms; we humans have no nature; what we have is a history.

Day 180. Nothing . . .

Nothing is more compelling than sexual desire and nothing more necessary than sexual discipline.

Day 181. The only time . . .

The only time people listen to me is when I say the wrong things.

Day 182. Cultivate . . .

Cultivate the art of silence and you may hear the still voice of truth.

Day 183. Man . . .

Man: beast most evil in places most civil.

JULY

Day 184. Eating . . .

Eating would be such a bother if God had not made it such a pleasure.

Day 185. Night . . .

Night is the hell of sunworshippers.

Day 186. They say . . .

They say Christianity is a fine thing. Has anyone around here ever tried it?

Day 187. Most people . . .

Most people grow old; some also grow up.

Day 188. America . . .

America, where people neglect their parents and obey their children.

Day 189. A sure way . . .

A sure way to change a nation is to lose a war—another is to win one.

Day 190. The pathway . . .

The pathway to our vocation is often littered with drudgery. Successful people are those able to survive it.

Day 191. Seeing . . .

Seeing through sham may not be the same ability as seeing into truth.

Day 192. Life . . .

Life is a gift, not a given.

Day 193. A person . . .

A person without enemies is probably a person without ambitions.

Day 194. Ambitious people . . .

Ambitious people might soon drive all countries to ruin were it not for us lazy folks who keep things safely mired in mediocrity.

Day 195. It is wrong . . .

It is wrong to make vice attractive, but worse to make virtue boring.

Day 196. God . . .

God answers all prayers, many by silence.

Day 197. We should . . .

We should be grateful for errors: without them there would be no progress—or need of it.

Day 198. The problem . . .

The problem with paradise is that you cannot improve it. At least that's what people tell us. But are they right?

Day 199. Paradise . . .

Paradise seems best suited for the lazy. The rest of humanity needs a realm with things to do and projects to complete. Come to think of it, don't we already live in such a world?

Day 200. I am . . .

I am extraordinarily patient and understanding so long as I get my way and dinner is on time.

Day 201. I wonder . . .

I wonder if we really need a devil? Hasn't humanity shown it is capable of every evil on its own?

Day 202. Moralists . . .

Moralists scold us for gossiping about people instead of discussing ideas. But don't they know that people are far more interesting? And probably you have already found out how hard it is to carry on an intelligent conversation with a notion.

Day 203. The Golden . . .

The Golden Ages of history exist only in retrospect after their protagonists died as mortals and were reborn as myths.

Day 204. Forget . . .

Forget what paleoanthropologists used to tell us about cavemen and fire. The real reason fire was invented was so men could see naked women in the dark.

Day 205. Truth in lending . . .

Truth in lending and warning labels: (1) pay us what you owe us, or you'll wish you had. (2) Drinking our beer will make you drunk. (3) Call your physician if you experience death or suicidal thoughts after taking this medication. He may be on it too.

Day 206. We respect . . .

We respect our forefathers for their virtues, but that does not mean we must repeat their vices.

Day 207. My idea . . .

My idea for getting rich is foolproof, that is, proof that fools will believe it.

Day 208. Strong minds . . .

Strong minds are not necessarily great minds. History consists mainly of the tensions between the two.

Day 209. When language . . .

When language is corrupted you may be sure that everything it serves is also in decline.

Day 210. We praise . . .

We praise undeserving people in hopes they will return the favor.

Day 211. If I had died . . .

If I had died as a youth, no doubt I would be remembered as a genius. Back then I knew everything.

Day 212. Death . . .

Death is weird; it happens to everybody alive, but nobody living can tell us about it.

Day 213. Old age . . .

Old age: the time when we finally discovered the secret of life but, alas, cannot remember now what it was.

Day 214. Every sin . . .

Every sin is an error, but not every error is a sin. Six months do not make a year, but it is not a sin to think so. Forgetting your wife's birthday is an error, but you will think it a sin when she gets through with you.

AUGUST

Day 215. A man . . .

A man indifferent to the size of his belly is usually expansively tolerant of the world's other excesses.

Day 216. He has dreamed . . .

He has dreamed up many great truths. Now if only he could find some examples.

Day 217. Our religious leaders . . .

Our religious leaders tell us not to break the Ten Commandments. But if we're going that far, wouldn't it be better just to go ahead and obey them too?

Day 218. Every great ideal . . .

Every great ideal is imperialistic but remember that some things are great without being good.

Day 219. These days . . .

These days they rank us by our IQ, or Intelligence Quotient. But what about our LQ, or Love Quotient? Isn't love why we were created in the first place and what makes the world go around? Is it too late to change the way we classify people? Intelligence seems too scarce a commodity to serve as the standard by which to judge people.

Day 20. Living . . .

As I look at life dispassionately, it occurs to me that living must be some sort of incurable disease. Doesn't everybody who catches it die of it sooner or later?

Day 221. Unverified . . .

Unverified phenomena: (1) UFOs; (2) Bigfoot; (3) An Italian who lost both hands but claims he can still talk.

Day 222. When . . .

When all is lost everything is free to begin anew.

Day 223. A Costa Rican . . .

A Costa Rican bus driver hung these signs in his bus: "Happy Adam: he had no mother-in-law," and "Married but not dead." I hear his life was short.

224.Which . . .

Which is the superior race? Personally, I would say either the Belmont or the Kentucky Derby, both run by horses. But rumors are that some of the entrants this year are real dogs.

Day 225. In many cases . . .

In many cases, those who will not believe the truth are no better at telling it. Skepticism wrecks many otherwise good minds.

Day 226. Many people . . .

Many people who live amidst beauty cease to notice it. It takes a flatlander to be awed by mountains and a desert dweller to appreciate trees and lakes. I wonder if people will become similarly bored with Paradise.

Day 227. Two heads . . .

Two heads are better than one unless one is better than two. Many projects are suited only to a singular individual talent. An eagle does not hire a robin to build its aery, nor does a Leonardo da Vinci ask a studio novice to help him paint the Mona Lisa.

Day 228. Hot tempers . . .

Hot tempers make rich lawyers.

Day 229. Freedom . . .

Freedom of speech affords no defense against the tyranny of opinion.

Day 230. Basic etiquette . . .

Basic etiquette: go when invited: leave before disinvited.

Day 231. Freedom of speech . . .

Freedom of speech: a license to deal in used opinions.

Day 232. How much . . .

How much more enlightened our world would have been if Descartes had said "I love, therefore I am."

Day 233. Theologians . . .

Theologians, scientists, and philosophers have always asked the wrong question: "What is man?" For it leads to wrong answers: animals, ashes, dust, chemicals, dissolution. The truer question is "Who is man?" Then follows the truer answer: "A unique creation in a higher category all its own".

Day 234. The dimensions . . .

The dimensions of our fear of death match the size of our doubts about life after death.

Day 235. Happiness . . .

Happiness consists in being yourself; but being yourself means becoming yourself, for we are born unfinished. Happiness is a journey not an arrival.

Day 236. A noted philosopher . . .

A noted philosopher calls happiness "the necessary impossibility," for even though we cannot live without it as our aim, neither can we forego it or proclaim it complete at any given moment of our life.

Day 237. God must . . .

God must love paradoxes: he created so many of them.

Day 238. We can . . .

We can thank the French for relieving kings and czars of the responsibility for wearing their heads on their shoulders.

Day 239. For their good . . .

For their good and ours, we must never elevate people so high that humor cannot bring them down to earth.

Day 240. Across the ages . . .

Across the ages, mankind has wavered between two competing convictions: (1) that what is new cannot be true and (2) that what is newer must be truer.

Day 241. Time and tide . . .

Time and tide wait for no man, but men have no choice but to wait for them.

Day 242. Duties . . .

Duties of a soldier and a diplomat: (1) For a soldier, dying for one's country is a patriotic duty. (2) For a diplomat, lying for one's country is a patriotic duty.

Day 243. Menopause . . .

Menopause: that remarkable period of life when women create their own climate.

Day 244. If I could . . .

If I could resurrect any of the old pagan gods, it would be Jupiter. When this happy giant was banished from creation, he took his jovial spirit with him, leaving the heavenlies awesomely righteous but dourly joyless.

Day 245. The Golden Age . . .

The Golden Age of mankind is history told without its warts and blemishes, like other obituaries.

SEPTEMBER

Day 246. Childhood . . .

Childhood is over when we discover that nobody really cares how much our bruises hurt.

Day 247. I have never . . .

I have never known an unworthy person, but I have met many whom I judged so because of my limited perception.

Day 248. How many . . .

How many accomplished people drive themselves to impressive achievements so that others will not learn they are the frauds they fear themselves to be?

Day 249. Creativity . . .

Creativity is the ability to complete what creation left unfinished.

Day 250. A Fable . . .

A rich man departed for a distant country. Word came later that he had died at sea. His family mourned for the customary time, then set about distributing his wealth and property and reordering their lives. His three sons received his lands and herds, his wife and two daughters his money and goods, and relatives and servants were rewarded according to their significance in his life. Then years later the man, now aged and worn, returned to reclaim his estate and resume his life. But despite his resemblance to their husband and father, the family rejected his claims. His wife had remarried, his sons and daughters were wealthy and comfortable, and to friends and relatives he was but a memory. He insisted but they were deaf to his entreaties.

"Our father is deceased," they insisted with a single voice, "and you insult his memory with your idle claims. Begone!"

But the old man insisted so loudly that some townspeople began to think that indeed he might be the selfsame man he said he was. His former wife was mortified, his daughters distraught, and his sons furious. They agreed that something must be done about the troublesome old man. Even if he were who he says, they reasoned, he has no right to come back after all these years to disrupt our lives and reclaim our inheritance.

Then following this reasoning to its logical conclusion, the heirs discreetly arranged for the old man to die a second time and leave them in peace to live their settled lives.

Moral: Room in this world soon vanishes for the departed, living or dead.

Day 251. Anorexics . . .

Anorexics look in the mirror and see themselves as fat. That must means I am also anorexic. For I look in the mirror and see myself fat too.

Day 252. I am an optimist . . .

I am an optimist: I do all my crossword puzzles in ink, but I admit they end up with smudges and write-overs.

Day 253. Only the fearful . . .

Only the fearful can be courageous, which is the will to stand despite fear in the face of peril. Courage is a high human virtue and the antithesis of nature. Most natural creatures live in a state of high alert, cowardice, and constant terror. Only the maternal love of animal mothers seems able to overcome it. Could that mean that human courage, which has a strong element of sacrifice, originated in motherly love, not in masculine ferocity?

Day 254. We are not . . .

We are not yet wealthy unless we have also acquired the time to make use of our wealth.

Day 255. In order . . .

In order to persuade, we must first seduce. Or if you insist, the other way around.

Day 256. Realists . . .

Realists who say they accept as real only what they can see, touch, and weigh surely do not realize the erroneous conclusion they have reached. Most of the human world is made up of abstract realities that cannot be seen, touched, or weighed. Some examples: mathematics, ideas, music, science, law, justice, love, logic, philosophy.

Day 257. Thought . . .

Thought explains the world; imagination gives it new dimensions.

Day 258. In our garden . . .

In our garden things grow that we did not sow. Both good and evil forces work unseen in our life. For everything we see happening in our life, much more is going on unseen.

Day 259. We understand . . .

We understand material things, abstractions, and animals by definitions, formulas, and descriptions, but in order to understand a person we must tell a story. Personal reality is in a category of its own that neither science nor philosophy has understood fully — and theology only in part.

Day 260. Nothing is . . .

Nothing is more irritating to great minds than strong minds that cannot be bothered with other points of view.

Day 262. Racial Golden Rule . . .

Racial Golden Rule: Respect every person; include no one because of race; exclude no one because of race.

Day 263. A Fable . . .

A rich merchant of old Damascus heard of a shepherd able to understand animal languages. Convinced that such knowledge would prove profitable, for everybody knows that animals can foresee the future, he hired the shepherd with orders to learn what the animals in his stables and pastures were saying.

That very week the shepherd heard a goat tell a friend that the merchant's most trusted slave would soon die. Whereupon he sold the faithful servant for a handsome sum, thereby avoiding the cost of caring for him.

Next, the shepherd reported that the cows told him that his prize stallion was about to expire, whereupon he also sold the horse for a considerable amount just before he died, and the new owner suffered the loss.

Soon thereafter one of his rams told the shepherd that the merchant himself would soon pass from this life.

The terrified merchant instructed the shepherd to ask the animals if they knew of some way to prevent his death.

"No," the shepherd reported, "all they can suggest is that you offer yourself for sale as you did the slave and the stallion. There is a buyer, but do not try to swindle him. We hear his retribution is terrifying."

Moral: As you mistreat others in this life, so you set the conditions to be mistreated yourself in the next.

Day 261. The Five Metallic Rules . . .

The Five Metallic Rules of behavior:
Day 1. Gold Rule: Do unto others as you would have them do unto you.
Day 2. Silver Rule: Do unto others in a way that honors you.
Day 3. Iron Rule: Do unto others as they do unto you.
Day 4. Tin Rule: Do unto others before they do unto you.
Day 5. Lead Rule: Do unto others whenever you can.

Day 264. If you speak . . .

If you speak evil of others expect to hear greater evil spoken against you in return. For you are a single slanderer but your slandered victims are many. The reverse is also true: do good and good will be multiplied unto you.

Day 265. Make up your mind . . .

Make up your mind: if a fox chases two rabbits he will catch neither.

Day 266. Begin . . .

> Begin no task, nor child beget,
> Till Friday end and moon be set.
> (Ancient maxim seldom observed)

Day 267. Learn . . .

Learn from nature: animals spend much of their best time preparing for their worst time. If we make no provision for the future, the future will make little provision for us.

Day 268. America . . .

America claims to the world leader in the advancement of human rights and the elimination of abuses. But are we really doing things right in this country when dogs have rights, but unborn children have none?

Day 270. Those who . . .

Those who set precedents have none.

Day 269. Travel . . .

Travel either broadens the mind or narrows the tolerance, but in either case lightens the purse.

Day 271. Many causes . . .

Many causes that men die for are not worth living for.

Day 272. If a thing . . .

If a thing is worth doing, do it with your might. If not, leave it to the deluded and move on to things worth your time.

Day 273. The greatest rivalries . . .

The greatest rivalries are not between competing men but colliding myths.

Day 274. It is easier . . .

It is easier to fight for justice than to live justly.

Day 275. It is a mark . . .

It is a mark of great souls to leave loose ends in their life work.
If I leave my room in a mess at my demise, will I qualify?

OCTOBER

Day 276. A half-truth . . .

A half-truth is a whole lie.

Day 277. Flattery . . .

Flattery is the art of telling others their fond opinion of themselves.

Day 278. Philosophy . . .

Philosophy does not provide definitive answers; it does something better: it asks stimulating questions, which is like tossing a new log on a dying fire.

Day 279. Do not . . .

Do not pretend to be wise in all things, at all times, and with all people; wisdom invites laughter and enjoyment. The truly wise are but children grown large.

Day 280. Do not involve . . .

Do not involve yourself with the secrets of your superiors nor cavort with the lax and lazy members of your organization, but with all people be courteous, dependable, and discreet.

Day 281. Keep three . . .

Keep three principles in mind when workplace troubles besiege you: (1) the best way to deal with an offense is to put it behind you, forget retaliation, and move on; (2) remember that sleep and time are your allies. What tortures you today will be less burdensome after you have slept, and time has passed; and (3) exercise and eat wisely; a healthy body is a strong corrective to an anxious mind.

Day 282. Mandated . . .

Mandated equality is legal at the start but impossible at the finish. We all begin equal like runners on the starting line; but the tableau breaks when the race begins, and talent and effort quickly separate us.

Day 283. Learning . . .

Learning is delightful to the wise, child or adult, but drudgery to the foolish, child or adult.

Day 284. Familiarity . . .

Familiarity is the most common form of blindness.

Day 285. No religion . . .

No religion gives instructions for making machines, doing science, or performing brain surgery. But a select few shed light by which we can see how to do these things.

Day 286. It is . . .

It is better to be needed than thanked. To thank a person carries a note of conclusion, perhaps of dismissal; to need someone is an invitation for that person to be more involved in our life.

Day 287. A Fable . . .

A young disciple challenged his master's authority, calling his doctrines outdated and unsuited for the new age. The master said nothing, but laying aside his scrolls, extracted a coin from his purse and handed it to the young man.

"Go, if you will, to the two men you see yonder repairing the wall and ask them the worth of this coin."

The disciple obeyed and soon returned with their responses.

"Master, the first worker said that the coin is bronze and worth no more than a week's ration of salt."

The master nodded and asked what the other man had said.

"The second man agreed with the first."

"Now go to the jeweler by the square and ask his opinion."

Soon the disciple ran back breathless with excitement.

"Master, he offered a thousand gold pieces for the coin! He says the design is ancient and bears the first king's very icon."

"Do you see the lesson to be derived from what you have learned about the coin? Do any of you understand fully?"

No one spoke, so the master explained.

"The coin was not valuable to the workmen, for they lacked the knowledge to assess it. But the jeweler knew its value and appraised it accordingly. You do not yet appreciate what you are learning and for you it still has little value. Only those who know what it really is can recognize its worth. This coin has been handed from one master to another since the Old Kingdom, along with the doctrines we learn here. In due time, the coin will be passed on to one of you, and also these doctrines to all here gathered. Now return the coin and let us resume our lessons. And remember that the doctrines are worth even more than the coin."

Moral: What is authentic and true remains so, and even more so, in every age.

Day 288. Relativity . . .

Relativity of human things: few things are more outdated than last week's newspaper, but after thousands of years the Great Pyramid remains the latest word in pyramids.

Day 289. A Jewish expert . . .

A Jewish expert on the Torah told me that God originally offered Moses fifty commandments. Moses shook his head and replied: "The Ark of the Covenant won't hold more than ten. Will that do?"

Day 290. As an adult . . .

As an adult I tried to reach the smokey blue of my childhood Appalachian Mountains. But the blue always receded before me into the distance, and I was left with the light of common day. It seems that some things—the horizon, for example— were created to exist only in the unreachable distance.

Day 291. Do not scorn . . .

Do not scorn trifles; they are the advance guard of reality.

Day 292. Usually . . .

Usually, childhood friendships must be reaffirmed in adulthood or else they fade. As our life pathways lengthen and veer off separately to our individual destinies, we have only a residue of old memories in common with our first friends, not future projects that will bind us anew. This is why, when we meet childhood friends years later, we often discover that though still friendly and affectionate, we are no longer friends.

Day 293. Americans have . . .

Americans have the custom of electing presidents whose most important qualification must be that they are unqualified for the position.

Day 294. A divine current . . .

A divine current courses through all creation and the cosmos vibrates with an echo of the Creator's original happiness with his handiwork. A sensitive soul will wish to be attuned to it and do its part in coaxing creation to plenitude, sensing divinity in the farthest world, the loneliest sparrow and tiniest flower, and recognizing the Creator's image in every human face.

Day 295. Human reality . . .

Human reality does not conform to abstract mathematical precision. To the eventual ruination of all deterministic tyrannies, it unfolds as a liberating narrative with subversive sidebars and rebellious margins.

Day 296. I bear within . . .

I bear within me many failed worlds wherein I could have lived and been a different me. But they said no to me, or I said so to them.

Day 297. This is love . . .

This is love: to make the perfection of your beloved the ideal of your life.

Day 298. Nothing . . .

Nothing is completely real until we can say it. The power of human utterance is a fainter echo of the divine words that brought the worlds and their creatures into being.

Day 299. Do not listen . . .

Do not listen to degraded music; only drugs and drink are more efficient at reducing the mind to idiocy.

Day 300. Miserable . . .

Miserable young wife: "I married this old man for his money. The money ran out, but the old man didn't."

Day 301. Do good . . .

Do good, if only a little, but often.

Day 302. Love . . .

Love requires our best if it is to survive, but sometimes we are not at our best. Love never fails us, but often we fail love.

Day 303. Please . . .

Please take time to clean your mind. If you're like me, your ideas have gone through a lot of heads, and there's no telling how contaminated they may be.

Day 304. The Rise and Fall . . .

The Rise and Fall of Generations:
The rugged father toils and tills,
His dainty offspring drinks and deals,
And shabby grandson begs and steals.

Day 305. Not every man . . .

Not every man is strong; but to be a man, he must have the gravitas that reminds us of strength.

Day 306. Women . . .

Women birth persons, men birth ideas.

NOVEMBER

*Day 307. Courtesy . . .

Courtesy refines strength; practice increases it, rudeness brutalizes it.

*Day 308. Ideas . . .

Ideas we never thought of may become ours if people leave them lying around unclaimed.

*Day 309. In childhood . . .

In childhood I was disheartened to discover that the word "fun" is not mentioned in the Bible but became more optimistic at puberty to learn that neither is the term "morality." At this stage of my life, I am happily working on what we do find in the Bible: intimations of redemption and eternities of life and love.

*Day 310. Free love . . .

Free love is neither free nor love, but counterfeits for which we pay exorbitant prices. In the marketplace of love the cheap imitations cost more than the genuine brand.

*Day 311. When . . .

When I first read about the "underworld" as a child I deduced with some confusion that a race of bad people lived underground, probably in the sewers of New York city. I had even more trouble understanding what was meant by the "New World." In church they told us that the whole world was made at the same time. I'm still not sure I have any of this down pat. I would like to see some scientific proof to settle the matter, maybe some soil tests, just to make sure that American dirt is as old as Egyptian sand.

*Day 312. Poet Antonio Machado . . .

Poet Antonio Machado says that at times he pauses to distinguish voices from echoes. Good idea: unless we stop periodically to recalibrate our way with reliable truths, echoes may mislead us with false readings.

*Day 313. Examine . . .

Examine what you claim as your main strength: it may prove to be your most dangerous weakness. We should check our conscience periodically for errors of judgment or pride. They are like weeds that sprout small but quickly become obnoxious.

*Day 314. We can . . .

We can truly possess only what we truly love.

*Day 315. Politics . . .

Politics: One of mankind's most remarkable forms of magical sleight of hand. It allows the few to control the many, comparable, say, to a poodle leading a panther. But don't we common people have the final power by way of the vote? Don't you believe it. As Mark Twain said, if politicians really believed voting was the key to power do you think they would let us common people do it?

*Day 316. Truth . . .

Truth can usually overwhelm lies, but it has its hands full with contradictions.

*Day 317. She would . . .

She would have gone further in her political career had she been more skilled at applying makeup to both her faces.

*Day 318. In former times . . .

In former times and in predictable rhythm, countries went to war. There were always official reasons to justify it, but deeper causes included ennui, stagnation, and most basic of all, a desire to test their strength and best one's enemies. The various super bombs, which supposedly elevated war to destructive inevitability, actually did the opposite by making war an act of insanity. But the result was a neurotic unease and frustrated hatred that has settled over practically all countries. Today no country admires any other. Most feel the need for an all-out war but lack the opportunity. Practically every country needs to go into therapy. But instead, all we have is politics and fanaticism. I think I just repeated myself.

*Day 319. Poor person . . .

Poor person, poor witness. Because poverty may make people susceptible to pressure and bribery; and their poverty may be the result of poor judgment to begin with.

*Day 320. If you . . .

If you would know the character of a man, mark the defects he describes in other people.

*Day 321. Empty Paradise . . .

Empty Paradise? All new revelations are heresies to older dogma and blasphemies of somebody's orthodoxy. Consequently, believers, old and new, have covered the earth with mutual condemnations of every faith and religion. Which begs the question, will there be anyone at all in Heaven? No, not if the Supreme Judge lets these human condemnations stand as decreed. Nobody has ever seen him, they tell us, yet word is that he is surprisingly merciful and may overrule these human anathemas. We must hope so, for if not, then the Kingdom of Heaven will be empty, and all humankind will packed like sardines in Hell. In which case we would have to ask, what was Heaven for?

*Day 322. Unfortunately . . .

Unfortunately, it is usually not the child but the teenager who survives when today's youth grow to adulthood.

*Day 323. The weakness . . .

The weakness of the proud: the inability to find worth in anyone but themselves.

*Day 324. There is a comfortable . . .

There is a comfortable companionship in running with the herd, but a higher consolation in going it alone if the herd has stampeded into error. The contemplative person avoids herds altogether and values as priceless the solitude that horrifies the mob.

*Day 325. Alarming headline:

Alarming headline: "Prominent senator caught wearing women's clothing." Then on page 2 you discover that the senator is a woman. But by then you have already wasted a dollar fifty.

*Day 326. It's a good first step . . .

"It's a good first step." So said a conservative lady when asked her opinion of capital punishment.

*Day 327. What offends . . .

What offends the ear offends the spirit.

*Day 328. Old Bob Bailey . . .

Old Bob Bailey is a happy man. He mowed the grass down by his barn and finally found his 1978 Buick missing all these years.

*Day 329. I have . . .

I have acquired some minor repute as a philosopher, but in all honesty, I was never very good at it. Bouts of happiness kept breaking up the philosophic morbidity I tried so hard to cultivate.

*Day 330. The doctor's . . .

The doctor's blunder lies six feet under. Medical quackery has a fascinating but horrific history of ignorance and butchery. French playwright Molière wrote some of the most scathingly comic accounts of inept doctors and their lethal practices in the dark ages of medicine. Does any of it linger in today's medicine?

*Day 331. Ad . . .

Ad in a Texas newspaper: Interested in meeting woman with bull. Send picture of bull.

*Day 332. Both my political . . .

Both my political representatives have encountered difficulties. My liberal representative is under fire for putting her head in the sand when it comes to ethical responsibility. But at least it allowed her to expose the personal assets that won her power. Meanwhile, polls indicate that many supporters of my conservative representative are disillusioned with his candidacy. It seems his wife gave birth to their child in a hospital, contrary to their expectations that the babe would be born in a manger.

*Day 333. Not every woman . . .

Not every woman is beautiful; but to be a woman, she must have the grace that reminds us of beauty.

*Day 334. Some people . . .

Some people are more interested in telling you their problems than in resolving them. Solve their dilemmas and they will soon come up with new ones.

Day 335. Even the best . . .

Even the best laws are inferior replacements for higher virtues we have lost. Virtues weaken and Laws proliferate in declining cultures. By 476 AD the sturdy Roman virtues had long since withered, but the Roman senate was still enacting new laws as the barbarians were knocking down the city gates and destroying the Empire.

DECEMBER

Day 336. Do not waste . . .

Do not waste your time with people who waste yours.

Day 337. If you . . .

If you would know the truth, heed less what you hear and more what you see.

Day 338. Some thoughts . . .

Some thoughts of wise Americans:

(a) If all people had the same opinion and ran to one side, the ship of state would be overborne and forthwith sunk.

(b) The bravest heroes are those who never fought a battle.

(c) You only live once, but if you work it right, once is enough.

(d) Do what you can, with what you have, where you are.

(e) Our only freedom is the freedom to discipline ourselves.

(f) The soldier, above all other people, prays for peace, for he must suffer and bear the deepest wounds and scars of war.

Day 339. Henry . . .

> Henry hasn't spoken to his wife in nearly a month.
> N0, they're not having marital problems that I know of. He just doesn't want to interrupt her when she's talking.

Day 340. There is . . .

> There is a symmetry in life: our ambition and ability usually taper off together, neither outlasting the other.

Day 341. Nothing so lovely . . .

> Nothing so lovely as new love won,
> Nothing so dreary as old love done.

Day 342. Philosophers . . .

> Philosophers: People who can look at the dullest of things and discover links to the most fascinating realities.

Day 343. There are lovely . . .

There are lovely flowers that have no aroma, and beautiful people who offer no love. Great beauty sometimes becomes an ego cult. Like the Greek god Narcissus, gorgeous people may be condemned to worship their own handsome reflection and pine away their life self-absorbed and indifferent to everything and everybody around them.

Day 344. Our strongest . . .

Our strongest truths are those we most resisted.

Day 345. I have developed . . .

I have developed a habit for living but can't seem to develop one for dying.

Day 346. Democracy

Instead of making people equal as it promised, democracy has made them envious, as wiser heads forewarned us.

Day 347. A Fable . . .

In an ancient kingdom a man respected for his wealth and wisdom pretended death to see how his family and friends would react to his passing. For he had accumulated power and riches to such a degree that he had doubts about the attitudes and adulation of those about him.

His wife wept and lamented her loss, then combed his hair and beard and straightened his collar, thinking already about the proper attire for his funeral and the adjustments she would need to make in household governance now that he died abruptly. The suddenness of his passing and the gravity of her decisions aroused a degree of resentment which she kept to herself.

His son considered the weight of responsibility that must now shift to his shoulders and began to think of ways to arrange affairs in the most beneficial way for himself and the family. He would need strength of character and clarity of thinking that he was not sure he possessed to a sufficient degree. He was disturbed but confided his doubts to no one.

His friends and relatives repeated kind words, remembered his generosity and wisdom, offered condolences to the family in their bereavement, and went on their way.

Only his daughter was openly distraught over the loss of her father. She spent hours by his bedside weeping and refusing food in her grief, and unable to accept the reality of his passing.

Then weary of the pretense and having learned what he needed to know, the father arose and greeted the household in the morning. A maid screamed and fainted, his wife paled, shed tears of relief, and then berated him for his folly. His son frowned in displeasure over the antic and feared that his father might losing his faculties. Only his daughter was ecstatic in her joy. The

Father, who had understood the thoughts of each and all, then instructed the family to gather about him and listen to his words.

"Apologies to all are in order, and accordingly I offer them most sincerely, but know that there was purpose in my deception that I will now explain: first, you dear wife, behaved as the responsible woman you have always been, thinking ahead and running the household in good form. I am pleased with you.

"And you, dear son, revealed the growing strength of character that I have often seen in you. I am pleased.

"As for our friends and relatives, they are too remote to be greatly affected by my passing. They acted as I expected.

"But in your conduct, dearest daughter, I perceived my failure. In the order of life, it is expected that I should precede you in death. However, I failed to prepare you properly but instead let fatherly affection displace paternal instruction in these mortal truths. Now let us all return to our normal affairs, and I shall try to alter your overwrought sentimentalities, dear daughter, with better teachings about life and death."

Moral: The truth about living is invalid unless it is also truth about dying.

Day 348. Great talent . . .

Great talent can be risky: crows live free; songbirds are imprisoned.

Day 349. Today . . .

Today freedom of speech has less to do with what we dare say than with what we dare not say.

Day 350. My mind . . .

My mind is like a steel trap: every idea I put in comes out mangled.

Day 351. It never fails . . .

It never fails. After all is said and done at our committee meeting, our chairwoman always adds an hour or two of commentary for good measure.

Day 352. Equivalences . . .

Equivalences. Is healing a man who wants to die the same as killing him if he desires to live?

Day 353. If we can . . .

If we can just make it through this world and the next, then maybe we can relax a bit and enjoy the scenery.

Day 354. Once upon a time . . .

Once upon a time orthodoxy stood for unquestioned truth; now many take it to mean outdated falsehood.

Day 355. The nearest thing . . .

The nearest thing we have to unpardonable sins are those we inherited from our forefathers.

Day 356. Sarcasm . . .

Sarcasm is humor's lesser twin: still laughable but not so funny.

Day 357. We . . .

We take lightly the conflicts of former ages because we are not compelled to fight their wars and resolve their problems.

Day 358. Well-fed people . . .

Well-fed people tell us that money is not all that important, but I have yet to hear a hungry person agree.

Day 359. He set out . . .

He set out to discover himself: unfortunately, he succeeded.

Day 360. Nothing . . .

Nothing lasts forever, except forever.

Day 361. He committed . . .

He committed political suicide and lived to regret it.

Day 362. It is unlikely . . .

It is unlikely that we will be faithful to large truths if we fail to respect small ones.

Day 363. We think . . .

We think we are being tolerant when we exchange one set of intolerances for another.

Day 364. Texas has . . .

Texas has the best climate in the world if you can stand the weather.

Day 365. We listen . . .

We listen mostly to those who recite the world's gigantic problems. Maybe we should begin to heed those who in small ways are finding solutions. The major calamities of the world are beyond our power to remedy, but we can do something here where we are, with what we have, and in our allotted time. Isn't it better to do what we can locally than to despair about what we cannot do universally?

Day 366. It is the nature . . .

It is the nature of humans to conceal things, which is why we wear clothes, tell lies, and have secrets.

Title: *Louisiana Rogue*
- Author: Harold Raley
- Publisher: Lamar University Press
- Paper Back: ISBN: 9780985255275
- eBook: Kindle
- Pages 306
- Publication Date: April 2013

This wonderfully entertaining picaresque novel by Harold Raley falls in the tradition of rogue literature established by Tom Jones and other early novels. Set in the nineteenth century, Louisiana Rogue will take you on a wild, fast-paced romp through all levels of Cajun society in the 1830s. The title page says the book promises to tell "The Life and Times of Pierre Prospère-Tourmoulin, Picket-pocket, Thief, Gambler, Fugitive, Undertaker, Barber, Doctor, Priest, Prisoner, Bandit, and Count; Latterly penned in his hand for the gentle reader of leisure, Spanning the years 1831-1839" and claims to be translated by Peter Tourmoulin.

Title: *The Light of Eden:*
A Christian Worldview
- Author: Harold Raley
- Publisher: John M. Hardy Publishing
- Paper Back: ISBN: 9780979839122
- Pages 196
- Publication Date: May 2008

The *Light of Eden* is the first book in a trilogy on immortality.

An inspiring vision of richer Christian life and thought. In the tradition of C. S. Lewis and G. K. Chesterton, this extraordinary book is both a spiritual adventure and an intellectual feast. Packed with illuminating insights and written in beautiful language, The *Light of Eden* introduces its readers to a vast treasury of creative ideas, innovative concepts, and possibilities contained in Christianity.

Title: *The Unknown God: Mysteries of Deity, Time, Space, and Creation*
- Author: Harold Raley
- Publisher: CreateSpace
- Paper Back: ISBN: 9781466273184
- Pages 142
- Publication Date: October, 2011

The Unknown God is the second book in a trilogy on immortality.

In his powerful Introduction to The Unknown God, religious thinker and writer Harold Raley makes this unusual request of the reader: "Suspend, if you will, everything you know about God. Put aside for the duration of this reading your traditional theologies and hear a new and more reverent way of thinking about God. When you return to your old understandings, they will have deeper meanings, unless those you once professed were meaningless to start with. If you are unwilling or unable to do as I ask, read no further. This message is not for you. The truth it contains will find you later when it is ready for you and you have been made ready for it." To approach Deity from this radically new perspective--arguably the greatest advance in theological thought of modern times--is to expose and shed light on the baffling paradoxes, improbable notions, and misleading errors not only about God but also about time, space, creation, and immortality. In each of these categories this book offers stunning new insights that incorporate not only the efforts of classical theologians but also the latest discoveries in science. Outline in these advanced insights is a new understanding of human life. By the law of corresponding identities, Raley explains, a more elevated theory of God necessarily means a more elevated theory of mankind. Each of the many themes and aperçus packed into this slender volume could have been a hefty tome. With pristine eloquence Raley reduces them to the essentials, believing as he does that clarity of style is courtesy to the reader.

Title: *Immortal Destiny*
- Author: Harold Raley
- Publisher: TotalRecall Publications
- Paper Back: ISBN: 9781590954430
- eBook: Kindle 9781590954447
- Pages 200
- Publication Date: 2018

Immortal Destiny is the third in a trilogy on immortality.

In *The Light of Eden* (2008) Raley invites the reader to a spiritual and intellectual feast featuring the mystery and reality of personhood and culminating in a new theory of human life. A radically new theory of life calls for a radically new theology, the main concepts and implications of which Raley explores In *The Unknown God* (2011). In it he argues for an expanded understanding of God, delves into theories of time, and offers fascinating perspectives of the Hereafter. The first two volumes of the trilogy set the stage for Raley's carefully reasoned but bold conclusions in *Immortal Destiny*. Summoning the discoveries of contemporary science, theology, and philosophy, Raley explores the dual modes of time and human life as creation, bodily reality, and survival. Raley peppers the pages of all his writings with rich perceptions and sidelong glances at many dimensions of truth.

Title: *Points Of Light*
- Author: Harold Raley
- Publisher: TotalRecall Publications
- Paper Back: ISBN: 9781590955369
- eBook ISBN: 9781590955376
- Pages 238
- Publication Date: October, 2017

These *Points of Light* centered on the beauty, humor, and mystery of human life present many perspectives flowing out of the unifying philosophical premise that life, not physical reality, is the foundational reality in which all others are rooted.

A noted thinker once said that clarity is the courtesy an author extends to the reader. Insofar as my abilities permit, I have tried to add another kindness: word economy, which I understand to mean saying as much as possible in the fewest words. In those cases, in which there is neither clarity nor economy, I alone take the blame.

Title: *Adventures in Language*

- Author: Harold Raley
- Publisher: TotalRecall Publications
- Paper Back: ISBN: 9781590955321
- eBook ISBN: 9781590955352
- Pages 216
- Publication Date: October, 2017

In these *Adventures in Language* linguist Harold Raley explores fascinating features of English and many other languages in different cultures and historical eras.

Even though at times I point out obvious errors in the languages as they are currently structured, I realize that the rules of grammar and usage in English or any other living language are, or can be, subject to change. This may not be true of, say, ancient Sanskrit, but then we note that despite its perfection—or perhaps because of it—ancient Sanskrit ceased to be a spoken tongue many centuries ago.

Over the ages thinkers have pondered the qualities that define humanity and set mankind apart from other species. In my view, no stronger case than language can be made for human uniqueness. Animals can communicate and mimic but they cannot speak. Language, sung, recited, or spoken, is archly human, and for that reason also deeply mysterious, beautiful, and fascinating.

Title: *Barefoot On A Frosty Morn*
- Author: Harold Raley
- Publisher: Mouse Gate Press
- Paper Back: ISBN: 9781590953426
- eBook ISBN: 9781590953433
- Pages 352
- Publication Date: October, 2016

Barefoot on a Frosty Morn is a literary and genealogical tapestry of several families over three centuries. The genealogical threads stretch back to England and France and unfold in step with America's continental expansion. The families crisscross north, south, and west as the tapestry grows in richness and complexity. A final episode sheds light on the earliest roots of the story. The reader has a perspective only partially available to the personalities immersed in the stories. Episodes are woven around some American milestones: the Revolution, the Civil War and WWII. These resonate and enrich but do not hinder the genealogical flow of the novel. In its conception and execution *Barefoot on a Frosty Morn* is unlike any writing before it. It surpasses the limits of history and narrates the essence of the American vision of life.

Title: *The Prodigal*
- Author: Harold Raley
- Publisher: Mouse Gate Press
- Paper Back: ISBN: 9781590953402
- eBook ISBN: 9781590953419
- Pages 96
- Publication Date: October, 2016

In the tradition of Crusoe and Sabatini, The Prodigal is a story of the shipwreck and struggle for survival of a young ship's carpenter who escapes one captivity only to fall into more dangerous circumstances. The story unfolds from Boston to Mexico, Cuba, Africa, and back again. At critical points a mysterious stranger intervenes to lend a hand and guide him to his destiny.

Title: *Memories of Appalachia*
- Author: Harold Raley
- Publisher: TotalRecall Publications
- Paper Back: ISBN: 9781590956496
- eBook ISBN: 9781590956052
- Pages 296
- Publication Date: 2020

A celebrated philosopher once said that in order to understand anything human we must tell a story. However, this human narrative is not about what we are. That kind of information is the business of science, which teaches us about our physical nature. But the real story of our life, the human portion, is who we are, and it begins where science and nature end. Biography, not biology, is the true human narrative.

No one can write our narrative for us, and no one should. For we are the novelists of ourselves, the composers of our personal melody of life. Daily we add pages to our story or notes to our song. Animals, our only flesh and blood companions in this world, are what they are by Nature's decree, but we humans are who we become primarily by our personal choices. This means that of all God's creatures, only we have the freedom—and therefore the responsibility—to choose how we live our life, and if necessary, to reconsider, to rectify, to repent and rewrite our story if it is sordid or change our tune if our music is discordant.

I take these distinctions to heart in this writing. It is the story of the things I did for the first twenty years of my life and what happened to me as I did them. In a general sense, this is the description of any life, great or small, and mine conforms to the pattern with nothing exceptional to recommend it. Mine is the unremarkable tale of an obscure life in an obscure place. Yet I cannot dismiss it as insignificant, for that would imply that I am judge and jury of life's meaning, which I am not, not even of my own life, most of all, my own life.

Title: *Tattletales*
- Author: Harold Raley
- Publisher: TotalRecall Publications
- Paper Back: ISBN: 9781648830044
- eBook ISBN: 9781648830051
- Pages 260
- Publication Date: 2020

A celebrated philosopher once said that in order to understand anything human we must tell a story. He spoke a profound truth, and it is important to understand some of its implications. Art, including musical and literary art, tells us very little about what we are. That kind of information is the business of science, which teaches that we are mammalian animals, first cousins to the great apes. On the other hand, art has much to tell us about who we are. It reminds us that we are persons, or better said, men and women, who daily add pages to a private narrative, or notes to an inimitable life melody. We are the novelists of ourselves. If we exist at a primary level as biological creatures subject to nature's laws and limitations, on a different plane we live as unique biographical persons whose mission is not to remain at nature's mercy but to humanize the world with artifact and artistry, creed and creativity, song and story. The thirteen tales in this book are modest examples of the high art of being human in a rich alchemy of styles, times, and climes.

Title: *The Spirit of Spain*
- Author: Harold Raley
- Publisher: Halcyon Pr Ltd
- Paper Back: ISBN: 9780970605498
9781648830167
- Pages 212
- Publication Date: October, 2001

The *Spirit of Spain* brims with aperçus and revelations, many of them controversial, others startling, all engrossing. From Roman Hispania to the most recent Spanish trends, Professor Raley narrates the unique story of Spanish civilization. Examples of his original thinking include a "phenomenology of Spanish history," a new theory of the Spanish Renaissance, new concepts of Spanish patriotism and nationalism, and a reinterpretation of Spanish "Stoicism." As the book unfolds he also takes many sidelong looks into Hispanic America and offers a new explanation of Spain's relationship to Moslem Al-Andalus and modern Europe. The book culminates in a radical analysis of "Quixotic life" and its unsuspected significance for the post-modern age.

Title: *Radical And Empirical Reality: Selected Writings on the Philosophy of José Ortega y Gasset and Julián Marías*

- Author: Harold Raley
- Publisher: TotalRecall Publications
- Paper Back: ISBN: 9781648830167
- Pages 276
- Publication Date: 2020

In this volume I offer the defining concepts of the philosophy of Ortega y Gasset (1883-1955) and his disciple and successor Julián Marías (1914-2005). Although these doctrines may be considered singly, they are best understood, so I believe, as a unique philosophic continuum with many junctures and cross references that illuminate and enrich both bodies of work. Marías describes his own relationship to Ortega as "filial," that is, "inexplicable without him, irreducible to him." Ortega cast his doctrine at the "height of the times," and in complementary mode Marías described his as the "depth of the times." I leave for others to ponder which is the greater thinker. I am too indebted to both to play favorites.

Title: Tides of Fortune
- Author: Harold Raley
- Publisher: TotalRecall Publications
- Paper Back: ISBN: 9781648830068
- eBook ISBN: 9781648830075
- Pages 202
- Publication Date: 2020

These are tales of fortune and forfeiture, happiness and hazard, love and deceit. Some stories are set in specific times and places but not confined to them. Others arise in the mere vastness of the world and belong anywhere applicable or nowhere definitive. For wherever there is human life, there are the yearnings, dreams, possibilities and impossibilities we call tales and stories. For this reason, I do not think of myself as their creator, but only their author or perhaps their channeler. I say this because the people who come to life in this book do not always behave as I wish and plan. I push and they push back. Which is why I am as surprised as the next person by what they decide to do and who they choose to be. Perhaps their way is best. For if the decisions were left up to me, most likely I would be their tyrant. As it is, I end up being their friend.

Title: Wit and Wisdom

- Author: Harold Raley
- Publisher: TotalRecall Publications
- Paper Back: ISBN: 9781648831263
- eBook ISBN: 9781648831270
- Pages 150
- Publication Date: 2021

These sayings, aphorisms, and moral fables represent many years of experience and meditation. They parallel in several respects my lifelong interest in philosophy, but whereas philosophy tends toward formal study and theory, the entries in this book translate the life of the mind into life as it unfolds in our daily problems and pleasures.

www.ingramcontent.com/pod-product-compliance
Lightning Source LLC
Chambersburg PA
CBHW050453110726
47899CB00003B/929

* 9 7 8 1 6 4 8 8 3 1 2 6 3 *